Little Bear Book

Thoughts, Dreams & Memories

of

_____

_____

Name

Age	Date

"Please write with me"

Coldstream Books

CANADA

Dedication

A friend
is one who listens
Even to the tiniest voice,
And responds with
understanding and compassion.

Little Bear Book

Long ago, there lived a very special bear.
When he spoke, his words were like magic and made people laugh.
One day he was given his own Little Bear Book.
"But," he said to his mom and dad, "I can't write yet."
"Don't worry," said his parents, "we'll write for you."
In the first pages of the book they wrote about Little Bear when he was a baby. There were also special pages for Mom, Dad, Grandma and Grandpa to write about themselves and about when they were young. At bedtime Little Bear would sit with his mom and dad and talk about everything he had done and felt that day. They would write down all his stories in the book and let him draw pictures. When the book was full, Little Bear kept it in a safe place so that it wouldn't get lost.

Many years passed and Little Bear grew up into a big bear and had a family of his own. One day, his daughter came running to him, crying "Daddy, Daddy! Look what I've found!"
"It's my Little Bear Book!" he said.
He lifted his daughter up onto his lap and began to read.
"Long ago, there lived a very special little bear..."

"Please write with me."

When I was a baby...

A Special Page
for Mom

A Special Page
for Dad

Family

_____
Me

_____   _____
Sister   Brother

_____
Mom

_____

_____
Cousin

_____
Cousin

_____
Cousin

_____   _____
Aunt   Uncle

_____   _____
Aunt   Uncle

_____
Grandma & Grandpa

_____   _____
Great Grandma & Grandpa   Great Grandma & Grandpa

Tree

_____

_____   _____
Sister   Brother

_____
Dad

_____

_____
Cousin

_____
Cousin

_____
Cousin

_____   _____
Aunt   Uncle

_____   _____
Aunt   Uncle

Grandma & Grandpa

Great Grandma & Grandpa   Great Grandma & Grandpa

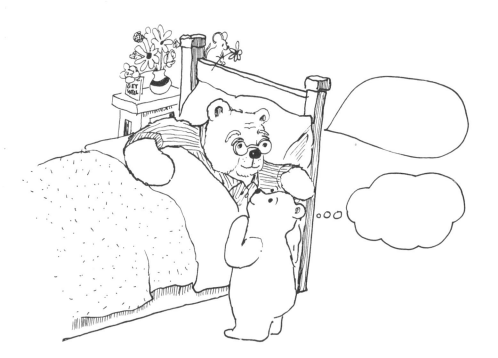

Memories of
Grandma & Grandpa

Memories of
Grandma & Grandpa

Memories
of Great
Grandma & Grandpa

Memories
of Great
Grandma & Grandpa

My Dreams
Are seeds of the future,
My Love
Is water which makes them grow,
My Patience
Is care with which I tend my garden,
And to share the flowers
In the end
Is my goal.

For Carmen & Gabriel
Thank-you for inspiring me.
Heidi

Little Bear Book
Written and Illustrated by Heidi Thompson

Copyright © 1994 by Heidi Thompson
All rights reserved. Published by Coldstream Books
9905 Coldstream Crk. Rd., Vernon, B.C., Canada, V1B 1C8
ISBN 0-9698147-2-0
Printed and Bound by Everbest Printing Co., Hong Kong